D1275153

Snail Saves the Day
John Stadler

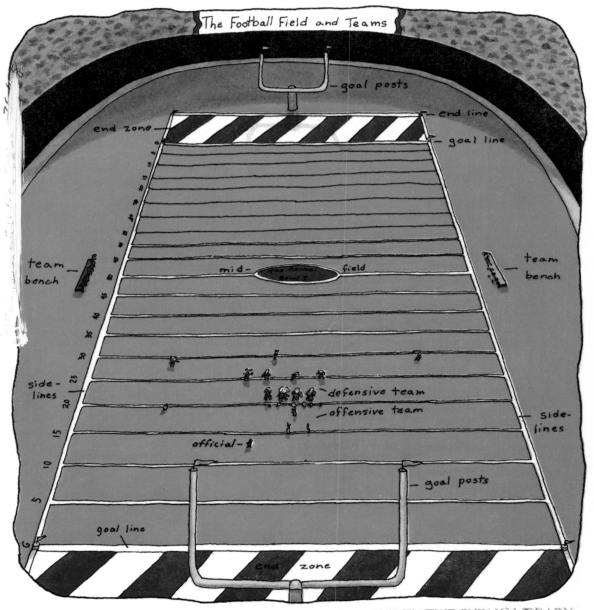

The Football Field and Teams

— goal posts
— end line
end zone — — goal line
team bench — — team bench
mid- The Animal Bowl I field — defensive team — offensive team
side- lines — side- lines
official —
— goal posts
goal line
end zone

Thomas Y. Crowell New York

Library of Congress Cataloging in Publication Data
Stadler, John.
    Snail saves the day.

    Summary: Snail's team may lose the football game
unless he makes it to the stadium in time.
    1. Children's stories, American.   [1. Snails—
Fiction. 2. Football—Fiction]   I. Title.
PZ7.S77575Sn 1985   [E]   85-47539
ISBN 0-690-04468-2
ISBN 0-690-04469-0 (lib. bdg.)

To Patrick Goldsmith and Hector

Dog talks to his team.

Dog has a plan.

The team lines up.

Dog gets the ball.

Dog is scared.

Dog is very scared.

Snail is asleep.

Dog runs away.

Snail wakes up.

Cat blocks Bear.

Snail brushes his teeth.

Dog drops the ball.

Snail gets dressed.

Rabbit has the ball.

Snail eats.

Dog takes the ball.

Snail drives the car.

Dog throws the ball.

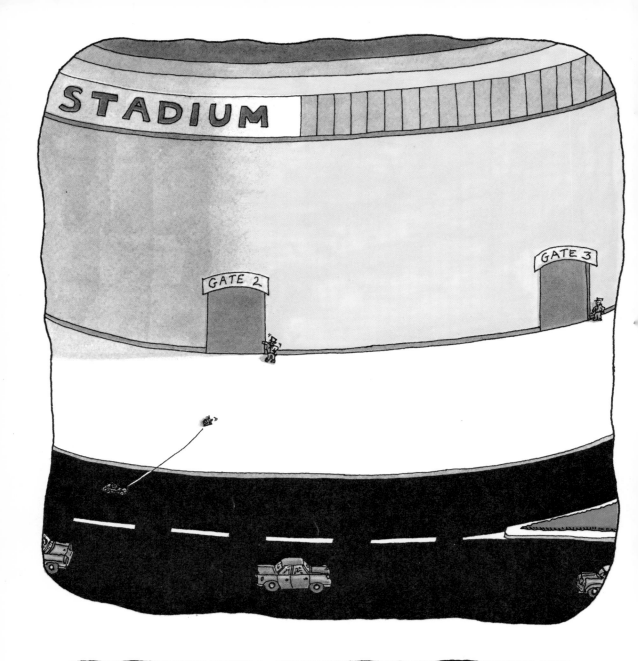

Snail is at the stadium.

The ball goes up.

Snail puts on his shoes.

The ball drops down.

Here comes Snail.

Here comes the ball.

Snail looks up.

OOPS.

Look out, Snail!

Snail catches the ball.

Snail wins the game.